The young man slipped the golden ring on her finger and they were married, and there was great rejoicing in their hearts.

At the door of the golden castle he dismounted from his horse and removed the cloak. He took the stick and touched the bolted door with it. And as quickly as the door opened, the raven, who waited inside, turned into the most beautiful Princess in the world.

The first scoundrel said he had found a stick that would open any door. The second said he had found a cloak that would render all that it touched invisible. And the third said he had found a horse that could go anywhere, even straight up the side of the Glass Mountain. They were fighting, they said, because they couldn't decide whether to own these possessions together as common property or to part company.

"I have a proposal," said the young man. "I have no money, but I have something more valuable to exchange for your possessions. Before I show it to you, though, I must try out these wonderful things you have, to see if you have spoken the truth."

The scoundrels' greed made their eyes bulge at the idea of something more valuable than their three possessions, and so they helped the young man mount the horse. Then they put the stick in his hand. Lastly, they put the cloak around his shoulders. No sooner had they done this than the young man and the stick and the horse all disappeared from sight.

"Don't you think it is more valuable to be alive than to kill one another for your possessions?" the invisible man asked. Then he turned the invisible horse and rode straight up the side of the mountain.

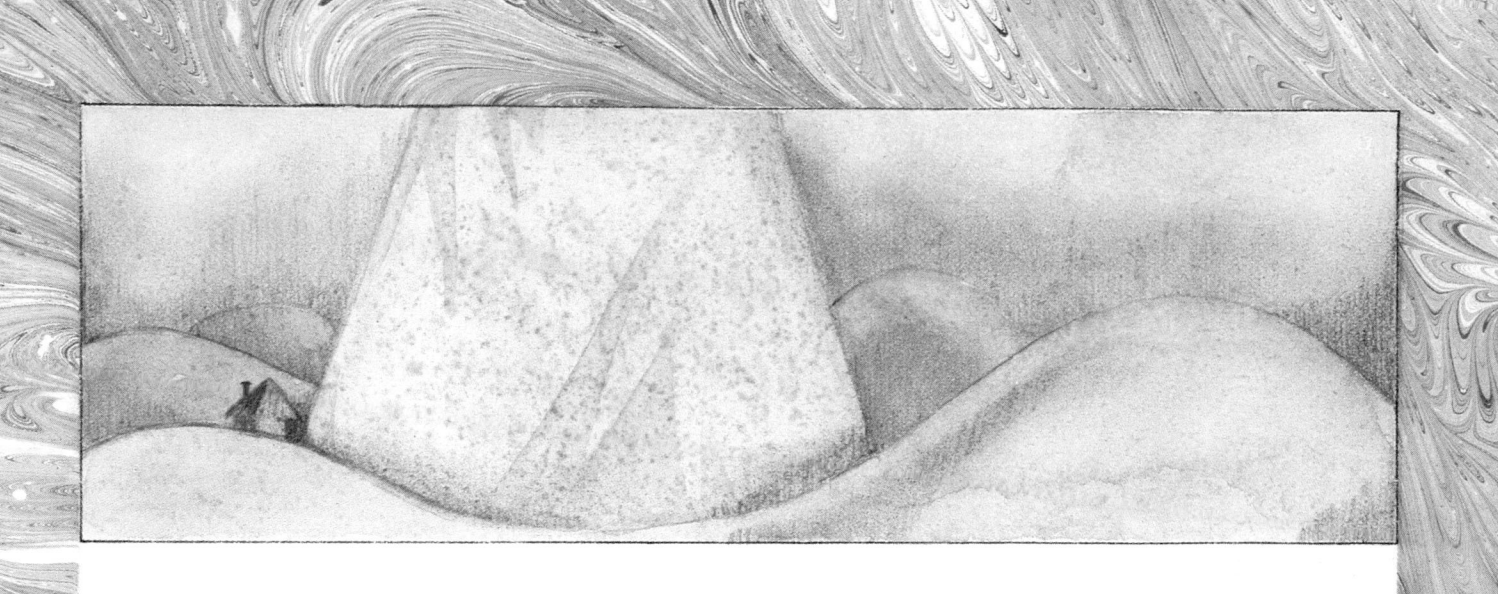

He knew the Princess was waiting in the castle at the peak of the mountain, and he was filled with grief when he realized that he couldn't reach her. He also knew that he would never leave her. And so he built a small hut at the foot of the mountain and waited there.

One day, on hearing a great commotion, he looked outside the hut and saw three scoundrels having a terrible fight.

"Mercy," he said.

They stopped for a moment when they heard his voice, then they continued fighting.

"Mercy," he said again.

Again they paused and listened, and then they continued to beat one another.

"Mercy," he said for the third time. And when they stopped this time, he asked them why they were fighting.

The young man went on, traveling day and night. He was overjoyed when at last he saw the Glass Mountain rise before him. He began to climb the mountain at once, but he slipped as fast as he climbed. He tried again and again, but he kept falling back.

He hoisted the young man on his shoulders and carried him over the countryside until they were within a few days' journey of the castle.

"You must go on from here by yourself," said the giant. He set the young man on the ground and departed.

He went into the house and sat at the table. The man laid out the food the raven had given him. The giant ate and ate, and ate some more, but there was still plenty of food. Finally, when the young man was certain that the giant was quite satisfied, he asked him if he could direct him to the golden castle of the Glass Mountain.

"I have heard of it," said the giant, "but I am not sure about the direction." He went to a cupboard and drew out some rolls of parchment and opened them one by one. They were detailed charts of all the neighboring lands.

The giant and the young man examined them with great care, but they could not find the site of the castle.

The young man prepared to leave, but the giant convinced him to wait for a second giant—his brother—who had some land charts of other kingdoms. So the man waited.

When the giant's brother returned home, there was another meal to be eaten. The young man laid the table once more with the food the raven had given him. The second giant ate his fill, then he, too, fetched his maps.

The young man and the giants studied each map until at last they found the golden castle of the Glass Mountain. But it was very far away.

"How will I get there?" asked the young man.

"I have some time to spare," said the second giant. "I can carry you to a place near the castle, but you must go the rest of the way alone."

He walked in the woods for fourteen days trying to find his way, but alas, he could not. And he became so weary that he lay down in a thicket and went to sleep.

He was awakened by a howling sound, and when he lifted his head, he saw candlelight. He rose and followed the light, and there, in a clearing, was a giant, standing in front of his house.

"If I take one more step," the young man thought, "the giant will see me." But he found his courage and continued walking.

"Aha!" said the giant. "I was just wondering what to eat. You will be a good supper for me."

"That may be so," answered the young man. "But it won't be as good for me. If it's food you want, I have enough to satisfy you."

"In that case you need not worry," the giant replied. "I prefer bread and meat and a good cup of wine."

When the young man woke up and saw that he had failed even a third time, his heart was very sad. Then he found the raven's gifts and read the letter which told him all that had passed. It continued:

Thus far you have not been able to lift the enchantment, but if it is your wish, then find me at the golden castle of the Glass Mountain. The food that I have left with you will replenish itself no matter how much you use. Remember, if you will it, I know that you can set me free.

The young man packed his belongings and set out at once to find the Glass Mountain. He journeyed for a long time and came to a dark forest.

Now it had been three days since the young man had eaten, and his hunger was great. After a time, the aromas of the meat and wine were so tempting to him that he thought, "A small sip of wine can't hurt." And he had a drink from the cup.

Then he grew very tired and stretched himself out for a rest. Once again, when the raven arrived, he was sleeping.

She had known he would be asleep. She called to him again but could not awaken him. This time before she flew away, she gave him three gifts.

The first was a loaf of bread, some meat, and a flask of wine, which she placed beside him.

The second was a golden ring with her name engraved on it, which she slipped on his finger.

And third, she had written him a letter, which she tucked into his pocket.

When the raven arrived, she called and called. But there was no waking him.

The next day, at noon, the old woman had prepared another meal for the young man, but he refused it.

"If you will not eat, at least have a sip of wine," she said. And she gave him no peace until he finally took some wine.

He went to wait for the raven, but he was suddenly overcome with exhaustion and could not stand up. He stretched out on the tan heap to rest, and when the raven arrived, he was fast asleep.

On the third day, the young man was even more determined not to eat or drink, but at noon the old woman came out to the garden carrying a tray heaped with meat and other delectable foods and a cup of wine for him to drink.

Although he said no to her offerings, she smiled and placed the tray near him in the garden. Then she returned to the house.

Before long, he came upon the old woman's house. As he turned to go into the garden, she saw him from the window.

"Poor man," she called. "You must be tired from your travels. Come and have some food and drink."

"No," he answered. "I will not eat or drink."

But the old woman was sly and finally convinced him to take a small sip from the cup she held out to him. Then he went into the garden and found the tan heap. His eyes were now getting heavy, and before two o'clock he was sleeping like a stone.

A young man was passing through the forest one day, and he heard a raven crying. He followed the sound.

When he came closer, the raven said, "I was born a King's daughter, but I was turned into a raven. If it is your wish, you can lift the enchantment and set me free."

"What can I do?" asked the young man.

"Go deeper into the forest," said the raven. "You will find a house belonging to an old woman. She will offer you food and drink, but if you accept even the smallest morsel, you will fall into a deep sleep and will not be able to free me. Behind the house is a garden, and in a corner of the garden is a heap of fir bark that is used for tanning leather. You must stand on it and wait for me. I will come to you at two o'clock each day for three days. If you can stay awake, you will lift the enchantment and I will be a Princess again."

The young man promised to carry out the raven's instructions.

But the raven said sadly, "I know that you will not be able to resist the old woman's offers."

Again the young man promised that he would do as she asked and thus would free her. And with that, he went on his way.

ONCE UPON A TIME, a child was born to a King and Queen. One day the little Princess was restless. No matter what the mother did, the baby would not be still, and so the Queen grew very impatient.

She stood at the window holding her baby as some ravens flew over the castle. She looked at her daughter and cried, "If only you were a raven, you could fly away, and I would have some peace!"

As the words came out of the Queen's mouth, the child turned into a raven. She flapped her wings and flew from the arms of her mother. She flew into a dark wood and stayed there for many years.

THE
GLASS
MOUNTAIN

THIS IS A BORZOI BOOK PUBLISHED BY ALFRED A. KNOPF, INC.

Copyright © 1985 by Nonny H. Kherdian

All rights reserved under International and Pan-American
Copyright Conventions. Published in the United States
by Alfred A. Knopf, Inc., New York, and simultaneously in
Canada by Random House of Canada Limited, Toronto.
Distributed by Random House, Inc., New York.
Manufactured in the United States of America
1   3   5   7   9   0   8   6   4   2

Library of Congress Cataloging in Publication Data
Hogrogian, Nonny. The Glass Mountain.   Summary: A man wins the
hand of a princess after releasing her from the enchantment
that has changed her into a raven.
[1. Fairy tales.   2. Folklore — Germany]
I. Title. PZ8.H687Gl   1985   398.2'1'0943   [E]   84-7848
ISBN 0-394-86724-6   ISBN 0-394-96724-0 (lib. bdg.)

THE GLASS MOUNTAIN

RETOLD FROM THE TALE BY THE BROTHERS
GRIMM (ORIGINALLY ENTITLED "THE RAVEN")
AND ILLUSTRATED BY NONNY HOGROGIAN

ALFRED A. KNOPF · NEW YORK

THE
GLASS
MOUNTAIN